How to Return a MONSTER

BY CHARLOTTE OFFSAY

ILLUSTRATED BY REA ZHAI

If you've had enough of that
fussy,
stinky,
parent-stealing monster . . .

Don't panic.
Simply prepare it for return.

Step 1: Find stamps.

They're usually in the
I-don't-know-where-this-goes drawer.

Step 2:
Distract grown-ups.

PRO TIP: The more complicated the request, the more time you'll have to prepare your package.

Step 3: Place stamp on monster's forehead.

Warning! This step requires close monster contact. Proceed with caution.

Step 4: Add more stamps.

You want to make absolutely sure the
monster gets back to where it came from.

Step 5: Transport monster to front door.

Along the way, collect waiting-for-the-mail-carrier supplies. I recommend the important things:

- ✓ Sparkly stuff.
- ✓ Snacks.
- ✓ Bouncy ball.
- ✓ Dance shoes (obviously).

Step 6:
Place monster
in mail slot.

Place monster
in mail slot.

Place monster next to mail slot.

Step 7: Wait for mail carrier.

And wait.

And wait.

And wait.

If your monster gets fussy,
distract it with sparkly stuff.

(Unlike parents, monsters appreciate a good glitter storm.)

Split your snack in two.
(It can be a little bit nice to
have someone to share with.)

Show off your dance moves.
(Monsters make a surprisingly good audience.)

Step 8: When you see the mail carrier coming, make any last-minute adjustments.

PRO TIP: Your monster might need:

- ✓ Supplies for future glitter storms.
- ✓ Snacks.
- ✓ Dance shoes.

Step 9: Remove your finger from monster's grasp.

If your monster won't let go, tell them they're going to be just fine out there. Maybe give them a little hug.

Monsters like hugs.

If your monster hugs you back . . .

and then boops your nose and giggles . . .

Step 10: Tell the mail carrier that this baby was delivered to the right place after all.

For Rick, who has never once tried to return me. —C.O.

For J, Katana, Yukiga, Carrot, and Bo,
who are always with me with tolerant hearts. —R.Z.

27 26 25 24 23 22 21   1 2 3 4 5 6 7 8

Hardcover ISBN: 978-1-5064-6469-5

Ebook ISBN: 978-1-5064-6888-4

Library of Congress Control Number: 2021937183

VN0004589; 9781506464695; JUN2021

Beaming Books
PO Box 1209
Minneapolis, MN 55440-1209

Beamingbooks.com

ABOUT THE AUTHOR
AND ILLUSTRATOR

CHARLOTTE OFFSAY is a children's book author living in Los Angeles with her husband and two small children. When she is not preventing one child from trying to return the other, she spends her time dreaming up and writing picture book manuscripts. Read more about her work at www.charlotteoffsay.com.

REA ZHAI was born and raised in China, where she developed a great passion for drawing. She currently lives in Beijing.